SHER SHAH

FARID, WHO LATER EARNED THE TITLE OF SHER SHAH, AND BECAME ONE OF THE GREATEST RULERS OF MEDIEVAL INDIA, WAS THE SON OF HASAN, AN AFGHAN ESTATE OWNER OF SASARAM.

HASAN HAD CAST ASIDE HIS AFGHAN WIFE, AND HAD MARRIED A BEAUTIFUL BUT WICKED YOUNG WOMAN, WHO HATED FARID AND HIS BROTHER NIZAM.

HASAN, FARID IS TOO INSOLENT. I WON'T STAND IT ANY LONGER.

WHAT HAS HE DONE NOW?

I CALLED HIM THRICE BUT HE WOULD NOT EVEN LOOK AT ME.

FARID TOO DISLIKED HIS STEP-MOTHER.

FARID! WHY DIDN'T YOU ANSWER YOUR MOTHER?

STEP-MOTHER YOU MEAN!

FARID!

NIZAM OFTEN HAD TO WATCH HELP-LESSLY THE ILL-TREATMENT METED OUT TO HIS ELDER BROTHER, FARID.

YOU'LL BE PUNISHED FOR THIS!

JUST AS YOU PUNISH YOUR POOR PEASANTS.

LATER—

DON'T CRY FARID. I WISH I COULD WRING HER NECK!

IT'S NO USE. FATHER IS COMPLETELY UNDER HER SPELL!

FARID WAS FIFTEEN YEARS OLD WHEN HE CAME TO JAMAL KHAN, THE GOVERNOR OF JAUNPUR.

YOU ARE WELCOME TO STAY HERE, MY BOY. I UNDERSTAND YOUR PLIGHT!

LATER· WHEN HASAN LEARNT OF FARID'S WHEREABOUTS, HE TRIED TO GET HIM BACK.

YOUR FATHER WANTS YOU TO RETURN TO SASARAM AND CONTINUE YOUR STUDIES THERE!

SIR, PLEASE TELL MY FATHER THAT JAUNPUR IS A FAR MORE SUITABLE PLACE FOR A SCHOLAR.

FARID APPLIED HIMSELF SERIOUSLY TO HIS WORK.

KNOWLEDGE IS THE FIRST STEPPING STONE TO SUCCESS.

4

HE MEMORISED SEVERAL ARABIC CLASSICS. THEN—

NOW I SHALL TAKE UP THE STUDY OF STATECRAFT.

THERE THE SYSTEMS OF LAND REVENUE INTERESTED HIM MOST.

THE POOR PEASANTS TOIL BUT DO NOT ENJOY THE FRUITS OF THEIR LABOUR.

IF I EVER GET THE OPPORTUNITY I WILL CHANGE ALL THAT.

THE OPPORTUNITY CAME WHEN HASAN REPENTED.

I HAVE LET MY WIFE INFLUENCE ME. I HAVE BEEN UNJUST TO A SON WHOSE ABILITIES ARE UNCOMMON.

HASAN WENT TO JAUNPUR TO MEET HIS SON. FARID WAS THEN 25 YEARS OLD.

I AM GETTING OLD. COME BACK AND MANAGE THE ESTATE.

HERE IS MY CHANCE TO PUT INTO PRACTICE ALL THE USEFUL THINGS I HAVE LEARNT.

BUT FARID WAS NOT ONE TO TRUST HIS WEAK FATHER WITHOUT CAUTION.

I PROMISE.

I'LL COME BACK IF YOU PROMISE TO LET ME DO WHAT IS JUST AND RIGHT.

FARID RETURNED TO SASARAM. THERE—

STOP THAT! THAT'S NO WAY TO MAKE HIM PAY HIS TAX.

I CAN'T PAY EVEN IF I WANT TO, SIR. THE YIELD WAS POOR.

THIS INCIDENT SET FARID THINKING.

HE INTRODUCED A NEW SYSTEM OF TAXATION.

THE LAND SHALL FIRST BE MEASURED AND THE TAX FIXED ACCORDINGLY.

WHEN THE YIELD IS GOOD THE LAND-OWNER WILL GET ONE FOURTH OF IT AS REVENUE. WHEN IT IS POOR LENIENCY SHALL BE SHOWN.

BUT THE OPPRESSORS RESENTED THE NEW SYSTEM. THEY RESISTED.

THIS YOUNG MAN IS A FOOL. LET'S IGNORE HIM.

IF WE DON'T EXACT MAXIMUM TAXES WHAT WILL WE LIVE ON? LET'S LEAVE THIS POINTLESS MEETING.

FARID WAS FURIOUS.

HOW DARE THEY WALK OUT OF THIS MEETING. THEY MUST BE TAUGHT A LESSON.

HE COLLECTED A SMALL BAND OF SUPPORTERS AND SWOOPED DOWN AT NIGHT ON THE VILLAGES BELONGING TO THE OFFENDERS.

SEIZE THEIR CATTLE AND GOODS. BUT LEAVE THEIR WIVES AND CHILDREN ALONE.

EVEN MY RELATIVES OR SOLDIERS ARE NOT TO BE SPARED IF THEY HELP THE OFFENDERS.

THE OBSTINATE OPPRESSORS AT LAST YIELDED.

WE PROMISE TO ABIDE BY YOUR TERMS.

HURRAH, MASTER FARID!

LONG LIVE MASTER FARID.

YOU SHALL ENJOY THE FRUITS OF YOUR LABOUR.

HIS STEP-MOTHER WAS ALARMED BY THE NEWS.

SULAIMAN, FARID IS BECOMING TOO POPULAR. WE MUST GET RID OF HIM.

THEY WENT STRAIGHT TO HASAN.

FARID IS SPOILING THE PEASANTS.

NO! HE KNOWS HOW TO DEAL WITH THEM.

YOU PROMISED THAT OUR SON SULAIMAN WOULD MANAGE THE ESTATE.

YES. BUT FARID IS VERY CAPABLE.

FARID! FARID! ALWAYS FARID. YOU ARE A LIAR. YOU DON'T KEEP PROMISES. YOU DON'T LOVE US.

THAT'S NOT TRUE.

THEN GET RID OF FARID. IMMEDIATELY!

NO! I CAN'T. I WON'T.

THEN I'LL KILL MYSELF.

OH NO... PLEASE... I'LL DO AS YOU WISH.

THE UTTERLY DISGUSTED FARID THIS TIME DECIDED TO APPROACH BIHAR KHAN WHOSE DOMAIN EXTENDED FROM JAUNPUR TO BIHAR.

IF HE ACCEPTS MY SERVICES, I WILL GET A CHANCE TO PUT MY POLITICAL THEORIES INTO PRACTICE.

BIHAR KHAN WAS ONLY TOO PLEASED TO ENGAGE FARID WHOSE FAME AS AN ABLE ADMINISTRATOR HAD SPREAD.

YOU SHALL LOOK AFTER MY PEOPLE'S WELFARE IN BIHAR. WE NEED SOMEONE LIKE YOU, FARID.

I'M HONOURED SIR.

IN TIME FARID BECAME BIHAR KHAN'S MOST TRUSTED FRIEND, AND OFTEN JOINED HIM ON THE HUNT.

FARID, ARE YOU READY? WE ARE ABOUT TO LEAVE.

THE GAME THAT DAY WAS A TIGER.

AH,! THERE HE IS. CAN YOU SEE HIM?

LET ME KILL HIM, SIR.

GR Roo R Roo

BRAVO, FARID. HENCEFORTH YOU SHALL BE KNOWN AS SHER KHAN.

AS TIME WENT ON, BIHAR KHAN BEGAN TO DEPEND MORE AND MORE ON SHER KHAN.

I APPOINT YOU TUTOR TO MY SON JALAL KHAN. MAKE HIM AS WISE AS YOU.

I SHALL SPARE NO EFFORTS, SIR.

MEANWHILE HASAN DIED.

THIS ORDER MAKES ME THE HEIR TO THE ESTATE. AT LAST IT'S MINE. BUT I WILL NOT LEAVE BIHAR KHAN YET.

A FEW YEARS LATER—

WITH YOUR PERMISSION, I WOULD LIKE TO VISIT SASARAM, SIR.

YOU MAY. BUT RETURN SOON.

MONTHS PASSED AND THERE WAS NO SIGN OF SHER KHAN. BIHAR KHAN WAS FURIOUS.

SINCE IT IS LOVE OF HIS OWN ESTATE THAT HAS KEPT HIM AWAY, DEPRIVE HIM OF IT AND GIVE IT TO SULAIMAN.

ONCE MORE THE ESTATE SLIPPED OUT OF SHER KHAN'S HANDS. NIZAM HAD A SUGGESTION.

WHY DON'T YOU ENTER THE SERVICE OF KING BABAR? HE MAY HELP YOU WIN BACK YOUR ESTATE.

A GOOD IDEA, NIZAM, A VERY GOOD IDEA.

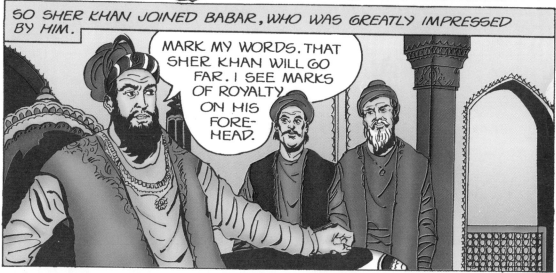

SO SHER KHAN JOINED BABAR, WHO WAS GREATLY IMPRESSED BY HIM.

MARK MY WORDS. THAT SHER KHAN WILL GO FAR. I SEE MARKS OF ROYALTY ON HIS FOREHEAD.

EARNING BABAR'S CONFIDENCE, SHER KHAN SOUGHT HIS HELP TO WIN BACK HIS ESTATE. BUT—

I CANNOT HELP YOU IMMEDIATELY, SHER KHAN. OUR POSITION AT THE MOMENT IS CRITICAL.

FIFTEEN MONTHS LATER, HOWEVER, DURING ONE OF BABAR'S CAMPAIGNS, THE ESTATE ONCE AGAIN FELL INTO SHER KHAN'S HANDS.

MY LAND! IT'S MINE AT LAST.

15

MEANWHILE BIHAR KHAN DIED.

A MESSAGE FROM BIHAR KHAN'S WIDOW? WHAT DOES SHE WANT?

...THERE IS UTTER CHAOS IN BIHAR. JALAL IS A MINOR. I CAN TURN ONLY TO YOU FOR HELP AND GUIDANCE.

FOUR DAYS LATER, AFTER SHER KHAN'S ARRIVAL IN BIHAR, THE WIDOWED QUEEN DIED.

THE TASK OF GOVERNING BIHAR IS NOW MINE.

HENCEFORTH NO ONE SHALL ACT INDEPENDENTLY OR GIVE ORDERS WITHOUT MY PERMISSION.

HIS REFORMS IN LAND REVENUE WERE INTRODUCED THROUGHOUT BIHAR.

I SHALL FIX THE REVENUE TO BE GIVEN BY THE PEASANTS TO THE LAND-OWNERS.

HE TOOK NO CHANCES WITH HIS PERSONAL SAFETY.

PICK OUT THE BEST OF OUR MEN TO BE MY BODY-GUARDS.

WITH POWER, HIS AMBITION TOO SOARED.

I HAVE THE PEOPLE'S CONFI-DENCE. I MUST NOW BECOME THE LEGAL RULER.

AT ABOUT THAT TIME AN IMPORTANT EVENT TOOK PLACE.

THE MASTER OF THE STRONG CHUNAR FORT HAS BEEN SLAIN. IT CAN BE YOURS, IF YOU AGREE TO MARRY THE WIDOW, LADY MALIKA.

HE AGREED AND THE WEDDING TOOK PLACE IN 1530.

I'M RICHER BY TWO THINGS — AN OVERFLOWING TREASURY AND A GOOD FORTRESS.

WHILE SHER KHAN SLEPT PEACEFULLY AND DREAMT OF FURTHER CONQUESTS...

...KING JALAL KHAN WAS AWAKE AND TROUBLED.

SHER KHAN IS BECOMING MORE POPULAR AND POWERFUL THAN I AM.

THERE WERE SEVERAL OTHER NOBLES WHO SHARED JALAL KHAN'S ANXIETIES.

SHER KHAN IS GROWING IN POWER.

THIS IS BAD FOR US.

WE SHOULD UNITE AND FIGHT HIM.

SO WHEN JALAL KHAN TOOK THE NOBLES INTO HIS CONFIDENCE, THEY GAVE HIM THEIR FULL SUPPORT.

I WANT YOUR HELP TO FIGHT SHER KHAN. LET'S UNITE.

WE ARE ONLY TOO EAGER TO HELP YOU FIGHT HIM.

JALAL THEN SOUGHT THE HELP OF KING MAHMUD SHAH OF BENGAL WHO HIMSELF COVETED BIHAR.

I'M WILLING TO HELP YOU THROW OUT SHER KHAN. LET'S BEGIN AT ONCE.

AND WHEN SHER KHAN IS OVERTHROWN IT WILL BE EASY FOR ME TO WREST BIHAR FROM YOUR HANDS.

THUS JALAL KHAN WITH MAHMUD SHAH'S HELP INVADED BIHAR. BUT—

WE CANNOT LET THEM TAKE BIHAR. LET US FIGHT HARD. WE SHALL THROW THEM OUT.

ON THE BATTLEFIELD AT SURAJGARH—

FIGHT HARDER MY BOYS.

HERE TAKE THIS... AND THIS.

AT LAST JALAL KHAN WAS DRIVEN OUT.

LONG LIVE SHER KHAN, DEFENDER OF BIHAR.

THIS VICTORY MAKES ME THE RULER OF BIHAR, BUT I MUST NOT ASSUME MY ROYAL TITLES AS YET.

LATER SHER KHAN RELENTLESSLY ATTACKED BENGAL, TILL, FINALLY—

KING MAHMUD SHAH HAS AGREED TO PAY YOU A LARGE SUM OF MONEY, IF YOU LEAVE NOW.

IN 1538 HE CAPTURED GAUR.

NOW IS THE TIME FOR THINKING AND PLANNING.

MY ARMY IS FIT AND LUCK IS WITH ME. I SHOULD STRIKE NOW. PERHAPS I COULD CAPTURE THE MUGHAL TERRITORIES FROM HUMAYUN.

SHER KHAN KNEW WHEN TO USE WORDS INSTEAD OF SWORDS.

MY LOYAL FRIENDS! HUMAYUN WANTS ME TO SURRENDER BIHAR, IF WE HAVE TO KEEP BENGAL. THIS MUGHAL HAS AN EVIL PLAN—TOTAL DESTRUCTION OF THE AFGHANS.

NO ! NO !

LET'S FIGHT HUMAYUN.

THIS WAS WHAT SHER KHAN WANTED TO HEAR.

SIR, NEWS HAS COME THAT HUMAYUN IS RETREATING TOWARDS AGRA.

THIS IS OUR CHANCE. NOW WE CAN CUT OFF HIS RETREAT.

WHILE HUMAYUN'S ARMY WAS GOING TOWARDS AGRA—

AT MY SIGNAL OUR TROOPS SHALL ATTACK THE MUGHALS AND CUT OFF THEIR RETREAT.

YES SIR.

WHILE THE IMPERIAL MUGHAL ARMY WAS SLEEPING PEACEFULLY—

NOW... ATTACK!

THE MUGHAL ARMY HAD NO TIME TO GET INTO BATTLE ARRAY. THEY RAN HERE AND THERE AS SHER KHAN STRUCK FROM ALL SIDES.

HELP!

OUR KING.

OUR KING IS INJURED. QUICK! PULL THE HORSES TOWARDS THE RIVER.

EMPEROR HUMAYUN HAS RUN AWAY. WE HAVE WON! WE HAVE WON!

BUT FARID HAD NO ROYAL BLOOD IN HIM—

IN ISLAMIC LAW TO ASSUME SOVEREIGNTY, THE NEW KING MUST HAVE KHUTBA* READ IN HIS NAME IN ALL THE MOSQUES, SIR.

LET IT BE DONE AND LET THERE BE FESTIVITIES FOR SEVEN DAYS.

IN DECEMBER·1539 A.D. SHER·KHAN ASCENDED THE THRONE OF BENGAL.

THE KING DESIRES TO BE KNOWN AS SHER SHAH. LET KHUTBA BE NOW READ IN THIS NAME. LONG LIVE KING SHER SHAH.

AMEN.

* SPECIAL PRAYERS.

KING SHER SHAH'S AMBITION WAS TO RULE OVER HINDUSTAN. AS LONG AS HUMAYUN WAS STILL THERE, HE HAD LITTLE CHANCE. SO A YEAR LATER, IN 1540 SHER SHAH'S ARMY PITCHED ITS TENTS OPPOSITE THE MUGHAL ARMY'S CAMP ON THE BANKS OF THE GANGES.

SHALL WE ATTACK NOW?

NO. THE TIME IS NOT YET RIPE.

HUMAYUN'S BROTHERS ARE NOT GOING TO HELP HIM. SOON THERE WILL BE PANIC IN THEIR CAMP.

HUMAYUN'S BROTHER HAS LEFT WITH HIS CAVALRY.

SEVERAL OFFICERS AND MEN ARE DESERTING HIM.

THERE IS CONFUSION IN HUMAYUN'S CAMP.

THIS IS THE TIME TO STRIKE.

FIVE DIVISIONS OF A THOUSAND MEN EACH SHOULD BE READY TO ATTACK TODAY.

YES SIR.

SHER SHAH'S MEN ENCIRCLED HUMAYUN'S CAMP.

NOW!

WHEN SHER SHAH REACHED AGRA, HUMAYUN FLED TO LAHORE.

GO AFTER HIM. DO NOT CAPTURE HIM BUT DRIVE HIM OUT OF HINDUSTAN.

YES SIR.

WHEN HUMAYUN AND HIS MEN WERE DRIVEN OUT OF HINDUSTAN, SHER SHAH'S SUCCESS WAS COMPLETE.

THE THRONE OF DELHI AT LAST.

ON TO DELHI. I'LL BUILD A NEW CITY.

SHER SHAH'S COURT—

IT IS MY ROYAL WISH THAT IN MY KINGDOM NEW TREES BE PLANTED; WELLS DUG AND REST HOUSES BUILT.

HINDUS AND MUSLIMS WILL BE TREATED ALIKE. ALL ARE MY SUBJECTS.

CRIMES SHALL BE PUNISHED, SEVERELY. I WANT MY PEOPLE TO SLEEP PEACEFULLY, WITH NO FEAR OF THIEVES.

COINS WERE STRUCK WHICH WERE THE GREATEST MONUMENT TO HIS MEMORY. THEY BECAME THE BASIS OF OUR EXISTING CURRENCY.

LOOK... ROUND... AND PURE SILVER! THIS RUPEE CAN BE EXCHANGED FOR GOODS.

ANOTHER OF HIS ACHIEVEMENTS WAS THE GRAND TRUNK ROAD, WHICH HELPED THE MOVEMENT OF GOODS IN PEACETIME AND OF TROOPS IN TIMES OF WAR.

THIS GREAT REFORMIST KING, SHER SHAH, RULED GLORIOUSLY FOR MORE THAN 5 YEARS; HIS REMAINS LIE IN A MAUSOLEUM BUILT BY HIM AT SASARAM.